Primal Echoes

Taila Cantrell

Contents

Dedication

This is the only book I will ever dedicate to myself. A part of me lives in the pages of all my stories, but this one... this one is for me. Come along on this journey and let us enjoy it together.

Trigger Warnings

Morally Black MMC

Primal Play

Hunting and Stalking

Choking

Murder/Death

Pregnancy/Childbirth

BDSM. Keep in mind that this is a work of fiction. If you are interested in practicing BDSM, please do your research and be safe.

Foreword

In a time, long before machines, the world stood still only once. Held its breath as two powers collided, creating a new magic. As the humans changed, magic did not disappear. It lived on strongly in two beings that were destined to change the very fabric of the universe. However, with change we must all adapt. The road ahead will span centuries. Fear not children, for they are with you.

One

Satarah

The forest was soft under my bare feet; the only sounds were the stream bubbling next to me and my own quiet humming as I washed the clothes Magda had asked me to clean. The sun shone brightly over my head. It was one of the first beautiful days since winter had come to an end Roaming these woods brought me a sense of peace. It was one of the few times I allowed myself to reminisce on my life. No matter how many years passed, my memory remained completely clear. That was both a blessing and a curse. To easily remember joy was wonderful, but pain was not easily forgotten. As I sat, staring up at the clear skies with only the trees for company I remembered the feeling of being terrified and alone. That is how I'd felt when Magda found me. I was but a small babe when she'd come across me, screaming out of fear and hunger. She had rushed to carry me back to her small village, hoping to find my parents. She'd had no luck. To this day we had no idea how I could have ended up so far up on the mountain with no sign of any parents. If not for the kindness of the village I would have perished. Instead, they had raised me, passing me home to home, filling my belly with food and my mind with their stories. I loved each member of the village like family; their joys and sorrows were mine as well. Magda was the most special of them all though. She had taken great care in always being available to me.

I repaid their kindnesses every day with the strange powers I'd manifested after my twenty fifth cycle. Strange only because I was the only one with any such abilities. I'd realized long ago that I was different from my people. My pale white hair didn't fit in well against the beauty of their dark tresses. Yet none of them shunned me for my differences. Instead, they had been excited as my powers helped them. I'd been able to work feats that made their simple lives easier. Mothers now lived through childbirth; our crops didn't die under the frost or the heat of the sun. Every new power I uncovered granted the people I loved another boon. My magic seemed endless, able to answer any need I had. It was primal in nature, instinctual. I was so grateful that I had been blessed so deeply. The only problem was I felt so empty inside. Loneliness was my most common companion. The humans my age were beginning to show their lines and wrinkles, stooping from a life of hard work. Instead, I remained unchanged. I still looked like I had when my powers first manifested. A part of things, but forever on the outside. I feared the day that death called for Magda, I'd felt the whispers of it, had laid my hand on her brow many times to stave it off. She was the oldest of the tribe, nearly eighty now. I couldn't forever hold off the natural way of things, but I wasn't ready to be completely alone yet. The small home we shared on the edge of the village brought me such fond memories. The feeling of warmth and safety was my only balm.

I sighed, finishing the final shirt in the basket. As I stood, I noticed the stillness of the woods. A feeling of foreboding raced down my spine, and I spun around preparing for a predator to attack. Bears and mountain lions roamed these mountains, always seeking their next meal. When nothing jumped out at me, I moved quickly. An instinctual part of me knew I had to flee this area immediately, lest I run into whatever stalked through these trees.

A darkness I'd never felt before. The feeling followed me all the way home. Even the next day as I set out to gather herbs for new potions, I felt the same darkness lurking somewhere. Some part of me knew that it would find me. Yet fear would not keep me from helping my people.

Two

Alcyoneus

My wings beat against the wind as I flew over the mountain range I had arrived at yesterday. I'd hunted, taking an elk down with ease for my supper. The stench of humans lingered on the wind, spoiling the peace I'd thought I'd found. I descended, heading for a small clearing in the trees. The moment I landed I morphed back into my natural form, feeling my magic flood my veins, pulsing along every atom of my body. I relished the feeling of all I could do. I had found no limit to my power yet. Since I'd slain my human captors, shaking myself free of the bonds I'd lived in for nearly fifty years, the world was mine to claim. I'd wiped out hundreds of human villages across the sea, laying waste to all who stepped in my path. I would hunt down the filth who lived on this land and claim it for myself. All humans deserved to die for the way I had suffered for they brought nothing but pain to everything they encountered. Their greed made me sick.

I shook away the rage swelling inside of me. Listening for any sounds that may lead me toward my prey. Strangely a pulse of power drew my attention instead. A power that tasted of honey on my tongue. I stalked toward it for miles, allowing the shadows of the trees to quicken my journey. I blended with them, moving in the blink of an eye. The pulse of the power drug me into a thick clearing of trees and a quiet hum met my ears. The melodic sound held emotions I could barely comprehend. A loneliness so profound it nearly brought me to my knees. I let the shadows coat my skin, keeping me hidden as I listened and waited. Patience had been my only companion in life. Years of hunger and pain had conditioned me well. I lusted for nothing; I could wait until my prey appeared. I had nothing but time.

I wasn't made to wait for long though. An angelic woman appeared mere feet from me. Her white hair glowed under the light of the sun. Her smooth skin was stretched over a body so plump and perfect it could have been sculpted from clay. From her perfect full lips, a sound fell unlike anything I'd ever heard before. The humming that conveyed emotions I had stuffed so deeply being faced with them was almost too much. I swallowed them all, moving to claim my prize.

"Woman, come." I boomed, appearing to her as she turned in my direction, "You are mine." She was even more beautiful up close. The dress she wore was sheer, giving me a perfect look at the shadows of her nipples and her perfectly shaped hips.

She didn't move for a moment, a look of fear flashing across her perfect face. When I looked into the bright silver eyes that stared back at me, I realized my mistake. A blast of magic threw me several feet away, sizzling into my chest and wrapping around my heart in an instant. The magic rolled through my body, leaving no part of my soul unturned as it ravaged me. I was frozen, staring into the sun as lightning struck my core. I couldn't even scream as she picked up her skirts and ran from me.

I had laid there until the sun set behind the trees. No one had bested me in battle since I was a child. Now the woman I had claimed as mine was also the source of the power I'd been drawn to. She was out there, alone in these woods. *Running* from me. My instincts urged me to track her, trace her. There was no corner of this earth she could run to that I would not hunt her down. She would be mine. I was more beast than man as I shifted to a wolf form. Finding a sweet scent that I knew without a doubt was hers. I raced over the terrain, ignoring it when human scents grew stronger. Until I began to see the signs of their village. Smoke filled my nose from the fires they had lit at each entrance.

I morphed back to my natural form. If they held my woman, I would tear the village down to find her. The pulse of power nearby had me stalking along. When a man stepped out of one of their homes I growled at him. A sword appeared in my hand without thought, the whistle of it through the air as I chopped his head off for standing in my way was music to my ears. I wasn't prepared for the screams of his family. I twirled, breathing hard as I stalked toward the mother holding her suckling infant. "Where is the woman with the white hair?" I demanded.

She sobbed as she glanced down, seeing the blood dripping from my blade. When she didn't answer I raised my blade again. The deadly arc was stopped by the slam of a glowing white shield. I almost breathed a sigh of relief as silver eyes clashed with mine. Instead, her power once again met mine. I grinned as we danced across the dirt, laughed when her fist slammed into my solar plexus. "You are strong willed and powerful, woman. You will do well in my bed." Her rage only served to make her more attractive to me. My cock hardened as she glared at me.

She snarled, "You will never touch me. No man who would cut down an innocent will share my bed."

I paused at those words, trying to understand how she could defend the human filth. In my hesitation, she saw the opportunity to disarm me. My sword flew from my hand, disappearing before it could hit the dirt. "Do you not feel the connection between us?" I growled.

"I feel nothing but sorrow at your actions." She said, her shield dropping away, "These people are under my protection. You will leave and never return."

I snorted, "You may so easily deny that we are one, but I see you for what you are. We are the same. Do you not wish to learn why we have been blessed? You allow these humans to control you?"

"They do not control me," She spit, "They are my friends, my family. Your carelessness with their lives is unforgiveable. If we are too be so different from them, it is our duty to use our strength to protect their weakness."

My mouth opened, but I could find no words to answer the rage I could feel pulsing through her body. My brows furrowed in confusion. The woman before me was no doubt my equal in every way. The only person on this god forsaken planet that might understand the powers that we seemed to share. How could she put these humans before me?

An elderly woman shuffled between us, "Satarah, please. Let us send Hona to rest with the spirits. There is no need to fight." Satarah. Her name was Satarah, I'd never heard anything so beautiful.

"He took Hona's life without a second thought, Magda. Cut him down for pleasure." She snapped. I could see the magic pulsing over her skin, white and black shadows twisting and angry as she stared at me.

"Look deeper. See the pain he carries. His death will not return Hona to us, but his life may be of use to you one day." Magda pleaded with her. I glanced down at the tiny, grey-haired woman. She was certainly the oldest human I'd ever seen. The scent of death clung to her skin, but I could see the white magic that laid over her like a blanket. My woman loved her, and clearly this tiny human sought to end our conflict.

Before Satarah could respond I shifted into shadow, transporting myself to the edge of the woods. I couldn't bring myself to go further, I was already entrapped by her. I would wait and watch until I made sense of Satarah. Then she would be mine. I would win her heart if that was what must be done. She could not escape me forever. I would follow her to the ends of the Earth.

Three

Satarah

I tossed and turned, unable to find enough comfort to rest. I'd had this problem every night since the dream. I'd found myself roaming an unfamiliar place that stunk of blood and death. The horrors I had witnessed as I walked the streets had been enough to turn my stomach. For a single moment I caught sight of the man who had killed Hona, the other magic user. Here he was not the impressive man, instead he was a thin boy, coated in blood and shit, coughing as he stumbled away from a building that burned. When a large human appeared and snatched the boy up by his hair I had looked away, but the sounds of the boy's cries broke my heart even now.

I sighed, sitting up from my bed as the man once again appeared in my mind's eye. His long black, hair shone almost blue in the sun. If he hadn't been so terrifying I would have called him beautiful. His purple eyes had taken in my body more like a beast than a man, and I'd known that running would only draw his attention more. If I had known what he would do, I would have let him take me in that clearing to spare Hona's life. Even though several months had passed, Yuma had not recovered from his lost. Their small son wailed all hours of the day and night. I had done my best to help, but for the first time in my life someone looked at me with hate and fear in their eyes. Yuma blamed me for her husband's death.

Had said as much when she had been drunk last night, praying to join their souls together again in death. My power had risen at her words, nearly granting her that wish. Instead, I had fled from her home. I was ashamed of my weakness.

"Come here, child. Have a cup of tea with me." Magda said as I entered our small cooking area. "You have not been sleeping well."

"It matters not," I waved her off, hoping to avoid this subject.

"You see him in your dreams. I have felt his presence in the woods. Ignoring the call, you feel too one another is more dangerous than allowing him into the village." I opened my mouth to argue, but she continued, "A beast cannot be tamed if it is not shown kindness and love."

"The people will never accept him." I pointed out.

"Maybe not, but will you allow our limited human abilities to rule your life forever?" Magda asked. When I stared at her in silence she heaved a sigh, "It is time I tell you the whole truth. Sit for I am an old woman and my memory is fading." I furrowed my brow but followed her instructions. I had never asked many questions about how I had ended up with Magda. It had never mattered. "I was only twenty when my sweet, Petra died. The grief of my daughter's death drove a wedge between me and my husband. I could no longer lay with him for fear that any child we had would suffer the same fate. Eventually, he left, seeking a new wife that could please him the way men desire." I growled low in my throat. Her husband should have stayed by her side through her suffering, for it was his to bear as well, "I am not angry with him for what he did. I had never loved him the way a wife should love her husband..." She trailed off, shaking away whatever memory had pulled her away, "In my grief, I had taken to roaming the woods at night. Begging any power in the universe to return me to my Petra." The sadness choked her for a moment, a stray tear falling down her face. I placed my hand over hers. Without thought my magic responded to her pain, easing it until she could continue. "One night when the moon hung heavy in the sky, I made a final plea. To give me a child to love. As I stared up, a star shot through the sky. Moments later your muffled cries greeted me. When I found you, and you stared up at me with those beautiful eyes of yours, I knew. I had been granted my wish, but you would be meant for great things."

We sat in silence for a moment as I processed the reality of her story. What power had brought me to her? "Why did you search for my parents when I young if you knew I'd come to you through this strange magic?" I finally asked.

"I am human, my girl, and the story of your appearance would not have made the elders of that time happy. They would have worried that whatever power gave you to me, may one day come to claim you again." Magda responded, "It was a necessary ruse until you were old enough to protect yourself."

"I could not have been blessed with a better life than the one you have given me." I said as I stood, pressing my lips to her brow, "I cannot leave you here to follow a cruel man."

"You have judged him harshly, Satarah. He was not raised in the love and acceptance that you were." She chided me, "No child stays with their mother forever. You were not destined to forever keep death from taking me."

I cringed as she called out my greatest secret so casually, "I still have much to learn from you."

"My sweet girl," She reached up, cupping my cheek, "I have taught you all that I know and for that you've blessed me with a long life and so much joy. Live your life for yourself. Do not let fear stand in the way of your fate."

"Fate will never control me." I said, "If it is fate that I bed a heathen, let it at least be one that takes the time to learn my name before he claims me as his."

We both laughed, and my heart lightened for a moment as I glanced into the fire. It danced in an unnatural way, my instincts telling me that I was being watched. I sent a splash of water into the flickering form, a pulse of power shuddering through my arm as they collided.

Magda made her exit, returning to her bed. I stared out into the dark sky; the stars seemed to wink at me. Their glittering secrets were a mystery to me now, but very soon I would learn exactly what they held in store for me.

Four

Alcyoneus

I was awoken by my instincts screaming that I was being watched. When I opened my eyes and found the woman that haunted my dreams standing above me, I didn't move. If she wanted to run me through, I would allow her to try. Neither of us spoke, giving me a chance to further examine her beauty. Across her cheeks and nose was a small smattering of freckles, an imperfection that somehow only added to her beauty. At this angle I couldn't help but look at the way her breasts hung heavily, nearly falling from the blue dress she wore today. I wanted to take them in my mouth. I would live to wring pleasure from her until she screamed my names to the heavens.

"Tell me how you came to walk these mountains" She demanded, studying me carefully as I sat up to face her.

I ground my teeth at her command. I didn't take well to anyone ordering me around since I'd slain my masters in the old country. "It's a gruesome tale that is not for a woman's ears."

She scowled, her silver eyes seeming to swirl in her frustration, "I am no mere woman."

She was right of course. No mere woman would make the blood in my veins boil with a single look. Satarah was the moon in the sky, and I was the wolf howling for her company. "I am old. Far older than I look."

"As am I." She responded in annoyance, "What does that have to do with my question."

"If I am to reveal my past to you, you will sit quietly and listen." I commanded.

She stared at me for a long moment before she carefully lowered herself to the ground across from me. It was the first time she had submitted to my will, and I desperately wanted to test just how delicious that submission would look on her as I rode her hard. I shifted, my cock responding to the images my mind had produced. "I no longer remember the first few years of my life, only faint feelings remain, but they were mostly pleasant. The woods were my home. Until I began to wander into human towns. At first, the humans ignored me, waved my desire for food, or comfort off. Eventually, it turned to fists and rage when I appeared. I was chased out of Romania at only twelve."

"What is Romania?" Satarah asked.

"It is a country across the sea." I answered. When the confusion remained in her eyes, I explained, "The world is a very large place, and humans can be found all over the land. A country is like a large village that is spread out over hundreds of miles. Sometimes they have kings that rule over them."

"These humans allow a single man to rule them?" She asked. I had not expected her naivety about the world. However, it made sense. If these mountains had been my home from birth I likely wouldn't leave either. There was a sense of peace here I'd never felt before.

I nodded, "Usually the kings have more wealth and power than the rest of the people. Not all humans are like the ones you know. One day I will show you the vast world we live in." When her lips pursed and she did not respond I continued my story, "I traveled alone for a couple of years, sticking to the wilds to avoid the humans. However, when I turned fifteen, I went into a village to seek the company of a maiden. That is where I met, Augustus. Somehow, he smelled the power on me. Called me a waer, and drug me back to his home."

"Is that what we are?" Satarah asked.

"We are whatever we desire to be. Do not let the humans define what we are capable of." I said, sitting up, "I did Augustus' dirty work for years. At first, it was comfortable. I made him gold, slayed his enemies… but greedy men will only ever become greedier. When he had conquered every village within a hundred miles, he turned his sights to something much larger. He wanted to conquer the heavens as well." I stopped, unable to continue. The years under Augustus' hand had been the hardest of my existence. I was only free now because I had brutally murdered his son. "I came here trying to escape the humans that have been nothing but a thorn in my side."

"I love the humans." Satarah said as she stood. "I understand why you feel the way you do, but I have never been shown anything but love by humanity."

"You have been blessed, and for that I am thankful." I stood, lifting my hand to touch her. I was surprised when she let me make contact. "You are a precious find, little star. I will be the sword that protects you for the rest of my days."

"I haven't decided not to kill you for what you did to Hona." She said, but I noticed the way she leaned ever so slightly into my touch. Something pulsed between us. A bond through our shared magic that I couldn't even begin to comprehend.

"If I am meant to die by your hand, then so be it. I will die looking at the most beautiful sight I've ever seen." I didn't know where the flowery language what coming from. Something about the precious creature standing before me brought out a softer side of me. I wanted to show her my devotion. If I had to learn to tolerate humanity I would.

"I will come and see you again tomorrow." She said, before turning to leave. I wanted to snatch her off the ground and steal her away to a cave I'd found nearby. Taste every inch of her skin, but instead I watched until she disappeared.

Satarah did visit me the next day. In fact, she had been visiting me daily for over a month. Talking about our lives, exploring the forest, and eventually she had insisted I come to meet Magda. The small woman was far more ornery than I had expected, forcing me to sit and enjoy dinner with them when I'd mentioned going to hunt. Satarah showed me more of her powers and I showed her mine. She'd even managed to teach me how she saw into the souls of the humans that surrounded her.

The beauty in her small village brought a new attitude to the forefront. Their bright, white souls called to an empty part of me. Like Satarah these humans had done nothing wrong. I still didn't like most humans, but maybe there were a few exceptions to my experiences with them.

"Come, Alcy. I want to show you my favorite place in the world." Satarah laughed as she drug me along. I cringed at the nickname she'd given me, but I refused to complain.

"Anywhere I am with you is my favorite place." I grinned back.

Something in her eyes lit up, a rush of desire I had noticed a few times before. My woman wanted me; she just didn't know how to handle it. I was earning her company, showing her that I would bend to her will. Soon she would bend to mine. I needed to claim her more than I needed air in my lungs. I would give her every drop of magic that lived in me for a single chance to explore the perfect curves of her body. I needed to taste the nectar between her thighs more than a starving man needed food. When she grabbed my hand to pull me along behind her into a small cave, I had to stop myself from pressing her against the stone.

With a flick of her wrist the walkway ahead of us was lit with soft, glowing light. We walked for a long time in silence. Until the cave opened into a small lake with a giant waterfall. The water was crystal clear as we moved closer. I'd never seen anything like it. "Do you want to swim?" She asked, a sheepish smile on her face.

I bent to take my boots off, but I nearly fell over when Satarah pulled the light green dress she'd been wearing over her head revealing every inch of her smooth skin. "Woman." I choked, "You can't tempt a beast like that."

She giggled, "The water will cool you off." She took off running, her ass jiggling until she dove into the water, disappearing for a few moments before her head popped up several feet away.

"You will be the death of me." I groaned.

"Or maybe I will be the reason you live." She said.

I paused, realizing for the first time that she was my reason for living. I had come to these mountains in hopes of finding a quiet hole to die in away from humanity. Instead, I had found my other half. "You already are." I said as I submersed myself in the water. I was surprised to find that it was slightly warm. When a tingle of magic flooded toward me, I realized she was using magic to heat it up to a comfortable temperature.

"Alcyoneus, I do not know what kind of life you had imagined for yourself, but I want you. I want you to be my husband. These last few weeks have been the happiest of my life." I was startled as

Satarah gripped my face, staring into my eyes, holding her breath as I considered her words.

"My sweet Satarah," I growled, reaching down to pull her body to mine, "You were my wife the moment I laid eyes on you. No power on this Earth could have kept me from your side." Husband and wife were human sentiments. They could never truly describe how we felt about one another. The pull to join had been nearly impossible to ignore. Being so close to her without devouring her had been torture.

"Let us seal our bond." She groaned before her lips crashed into mine. The taste of honey and citrus filled my senses. I lifted her in the water until she wrapped her legs around my waist. Magic flared from us as I deepened the kiss. When I pulled away, her pupils were blown out until the silver was almost gone, "Please take me."

I growled, nearly running toward the shore. I kicked our clothes into a pile before I carefully laid her down on top of them. "Show me what belongs to me, little star."

She moaned as she spread her legs, revealing her pussy. Already swollen from her desire I knew I could have plunged into her without another thought, but I stopped myself. Our first time would be something she'd never forget. I ran my hands over her creamy thighs, but she stopped me, "If you don't rut me right now, I will die."

I laughed, "You are not in charge now, Satarah. When we are to be man and wife you will only do as I say. Your pleasure is mine to control." Her eyes widened and I noticed her pussy starting to glisten, "You like that don't you? You know exactly who you belong to. Maybe if you beg I will take mercy on you."

"Maybe you don't know what you're doing." She was going to continue speaking, but my hand wrapped around her throat cutting off her air as I lifted her body, turning her until she faced away from me. Without thought my hand smacked the perfect globe of her ass. When she moaned I did it again. I didn't stop until her ass was glowing red in the dim light. Finally, I slid my fingers lower, into her dripping pussy. She gasped as I crooked my fingers, pressing deeply into the spot that would bring her over the edge.

"Will you find your release on my fingers with a smarting ass?" I teased her for another moment, "No I think I will find my release first, deep inside of you where my seed belongs."

"Please." She begged, and I could not take another moment outside of her. I lined myself up with her slick entrance, entering her in a single motion.

For a single moment the cavern around us shook. I knew in a deep part of my soul that the entire world had felt the moment I joined with Satarah. As I pounded my cock deeper into her perfect channel I felt the world pause. In that pause we delved deeper into one another, my teeth biting down into her neck as I played with her clit. Every part of our bodies connected. When I felt her muscles tighten, my release grew, and we cried out together. Deep purple magic shooting in every direction as we rode our high together. I was careful not to collapse on her smaller body, pulling her into my chest. The sound of our pants filled the cavernous space, and I felt the moment the world began to spin again. My soul settled for the first time in my life. I felt the bond between us like a limb, bright and burning.

"I love you." Satarah whispered into my chest.

"Love is not a strong enough word for what I feel for you, little star. You are my heart, beating outside of my chest. My greatest weakness and my greatest strength. No, I do not love you. I long to be one with you for eternity." I said, pressing my lips into her wet hair. I hadn't even noticed the water dripping off of us until now. With a wave of my hand, I dried us and our clothes off. "Let us return to Magda. I seek her guidance in human martial vows."

Five

Satarah

Alcyoneus and I built our own small home on the edge of the village. Far enough away that my husband didn't have to deal with the humans overly often, but close enough that I could easily assist anyone. A small one room hut was all that we needed for now. We spent more time tangled in each other's bodies than doing anything else. Magda visited most days for lunch, so when lunch came and went with no sign of her worry churned in my stomach. Something was terribly wrong.

"I'm sure she's fine, my sweet. You know how hard it is for the elderly humans to get around." Alcyoneus said as I paced across the floor.

"I'm going to go check on her." I insisted.

"I'll go with you. Stretching my legs sounds nice." He said as we made our way toward the village.

The smell of smoke greeted me as we turned the bend to enter the village. I ran the moment I heard the sounds of screams. The chaos as we entered the epicenter of violence was enough to make my head spin. Bodies were littered all over the ground. Men, women and children had been eviscerated without thought. My magic responded to my horror, lashing out at a man wearing a strange metal helmet. "Who are you?" I growled, ripping the helmet from his head to reveal the pale face of a young boy.

Whatever language he spoke I didn't understand, but Alcyoneus stepped forward, "He's from the old country, little star. The devils have found our home."

Without a thought a short dagger appeared in my hand, and I beheaded the boy. I dropped his body to the ground, "Find them all, make them pay for what they have done." I commanded.

A grin unlike any I had ever seen before curled across my husband's face, "Your every desire is mine to fulfill. I shall take much joy in ensuring that they suffer."

He kissed me, not caring for the blood that had sprayed across my face. It was smeared across his when he pulled away, disappearing into shadows as I picked my way over the land seeking any survivors. Thankfully, several of men had herded the women into a single space, protecting them with their lives. I sent them to our home, promising to avenge the deaths of our people. Every being I came across was friend or foe. Friends were sent to my home, while I slaughtered our enemies. I had never thought I would relish in the deaths of others, but the feeling of vengeance followed me until I came to Magda's smoldering home.

"Magda." I shouted. I called my magic, seeking her through shadows. I found her soul dimmed, but still alive. I rushed to the spot, finding her body discarded beside several dead men.

"My sweet Satarah." She mumbled as I lifted her frail body into my arms, "Raising you was the best part of my long life."

"It's not over yet." I cried, calling my magic. I would find a way to keep her alive.

"No child. Let me pass on. We will be together again someday." She coughed, wheezing.

"I can't live without you." Rage and grief filled me. These careless humans had taken the only mother I had ever known. "This is not how it is supposed to be." Magic rolled from me in waves as Magda took her final breath, words leaving my mouth without thoughts, "My people will never suffer defenseless at the hands of humans again. I grant them the powers they deserve to defend themselves and the purity of humanity henceforth."

I glanced down tears blurring my vision as Magda took her final labored breaths. That was how Alcyoneus found me, panic in his eyes, "What have you done?"

"None of my people will ever suffer at the hands of that filth again." I said, standing with the only mother I'd ever known in my arms, "They will be called witches, and we shall look over them."

"The males are mine," He growled, "What power you granted them was ours to give. The males will be called warlocks."

"So shall it be." I nodded. We walked in silence, tears still running down my face as we made our way back to our home.

The people gathered there bowed as we approached. Colors of all kinds surrounded their once white auras. I could feel the magic that I had blessed them with reach out to me. "Today you have become different. You and those like you will be tasked with protecting the humans with pure souls. Tonight, we will bury our dead, scream your rage to the heavens. Tomorrow we will find the filth that walks our land and wipe them out."

Cries went up, chants and shouts meeting my ears. I heard none of it as I continued to walk until I came to the small meadow Magda had found me in all those years ago. I used my power to open the earth. I stood staring into the hole still holding her body for a long moment. I pressed my lips to her forehead, smoothing her grey hair from her face, "Thank you, mother. Rest peacefully now. One day we will be reunited."

I laid her in the hole carefully. Eventually I closed it, and yellow flowers sprung up where her body laid. I sat down, my tears spent but my grief an open chasm in my chest. Magda had led me through life, and I didn't know how to move on without her.

"Come wife. It is time to rest." Alcyoneus' voice interrupted my mourning. "Magda was the best of humans. Her memory will live on for all eternity. Let us rest so that we might lead our witches in the light of a new day." He pulled me from the ground, crushing me into his chest. The tears flowed freely down my face as I screamed my rage into him. He took every bit of it without complaint, holding me tightly until I collapsed. Then he carried me gently back to our home promising me that tomorrow was the dawn of a new era.

Six

Alcyoneus

Satarah was no longer satisfied to sit in our home and enjoy the quiet peace of our village. She had left an elder in charge of our newly anointed witches, promising to return soon. As we made our way across the land, we brought death to those that sought to harm. What we found was that Satarah's magic had not just granted her people magic, but instead hundreds of humans across the globe had been changed. We would be responsible for spreading the message about their powers, but right now my wife was still set on vengeance.

Even as she rode my cock, breasts bouncing in my face I saw the rage simmering in her eyes. I had basked in it at first, enjoying her feral infuriation. However, as I stared up at her now, I realized that the pain she carried would never be fixed by slaughtering humans. In that moment, I made a decision. Sitting up, I wrapped my hand around her slender neck, squeezing until she became limp in my arms, "Little star, tonight I will rid you of your pent-up emotion."

"Just give me your cock, husband." She demanded under my fist.

I ignored her, rearranging us until she was on her knees with her face pressed against the bedroll. I took in her perfect body for a long moment. I would never tire of her voluptuous curves, the freckles across the tops of her shoulders, or the way she screamed when I took her ass. Finally, an idea formed in my mind, and I called for my magic. Shadows slithered across the ground, wrapping around her ankles, wrists, and neck until she was held immobile before me. "There is no part of you that I do not desire. Tonight, I will revel in every inch of you, pushing you far past your limits. You will break for me, and when I am done you will thank me."

I saw defiance in her eyes, but soon she would think of nothing but my hands on her body. I started simply, pinching her clit, while one of my shadows opened her ass for me. Her hips gyrated, but I added more shadows forcing her to still. She would receive no pleasure from me until I had wrung her rage dry. When she was broken in my arms, I would rebuild her with pleasure. My woman would not suffer for anyone but me. I called ice to my fingers, and she screamed as I plunged those cold digits into her dripping pussy. I relished the sounds of her cries, my cock hardening to the point of pain. Instead, I called more magic, muffling her screams so that no humans would come searching. Her noises were for me alone. When her body shook, desperate to collapse I pushed further. Her ass was full of my shadows, so I rained slaps across it's globes. The red shone brightly against her skin, complimenting the paleness. I took in her tear-streaked face, and I couldn't stop myself from leaning toward and licking the tears away. Her white hair was tangled around her, so I gathered it into my fist forcing her head up, "My perfect wife. Your pussy is begging to be filled with my seed. Beg me for what you truly desire."

I pulled the magic away from her mouth, "Alcyoneus please... Use my body. Make me forget."

I pressed a kiss to her lips before I once again rearranged her using shadows. Now she was suspended in the air. Spread wide before me, her juices dripping down her thighs. I commanded more shadows to her ass, filling her hole until I saw the pain in her eyes. Her breasts heaved with every thrust of magic into her, and I could not stop myself from taking them into my hands. I rolled her pink nipples between my fingers, ruthlessly tugging until her eyes rolled back into her head from the pleasure that the pain brought her.

So finally, I sunk my cock deep inside of her. The shadows did not stop their relentless use of her ass causing her pussy to squeeze me almost painfully. I began a punishing pace, snapping my hips into her with such force that the shadows surrounding us shivered. When my body tightened with my impending orgasm I reached down, rubbing circles around her sensitive bud until a scream so primal left her throat that the ground around us shook. My own scream followed, and I released all the magic I'd been using. Tears fell onto my chest as the shadows disappeared, leaving my perfect wife shaking in my arms. I gathered her up, sitting her in my lap with my back against the tent. She stayed like that, crying and shaking until finally her swirling silver eyes met mine, "Thank you, husband."

"I will fulfill your every need, wife. Even when you don't know exactly what it is you need." I said.

"For the first time, I understand why you killed Hona. The humans with tainted souls deserve nothing but death." She admitted, "How have you moved past it all?"

"I found something I wanted more than revenge." I said as I began to braid her hair, fixing the damage we'd done to it. "What the humans took from you is tragic. Magda was a truly pure soul, but she would not want you to avenge her in this way. Let us return home, we do not have to stay there, but our witches need our guidance."

"How will the witches all over the world learn to follow the way we've paved for them?" Satarah mused as we moved back to our bedroll.

"I have a few ideas, but they can wait until morning. For now you must rest." I said, gathering her against my body until her quiet snores lulled me into slumber.

Within hours of reappearing in our small village, Satarah had called a meeting of all the witches in the area. Now she paced the ground, waiting for everyone to arrive. "Are you sure giving them laws to follow is the best route. If they break the laws that we give them, we'll be forced to punish them."

"They are reasonable and simple rules to live by. If they cannot follow them, then they should not have the power to begin with." I offered, trying to ease her anxiety.

"And covens? Are you sure that giving them a way to even more power is a good plan. I don't want them to be targeted by humans." She chewed on one of her nails as she spoke.

"We cannot be everywhere, little star. They need a coven so that an elder can guide them on the path we've chosen for them." I said, standing and stopping her in her tracks, "Stop worrying. If they cannot follow our path, I will strip them of their powers and their lives."

She nodded. Together, we stepped out of our small home finding a sea of people waiting for us. Far more than had been here the day that Satarah had granted them power. Clearly, the new witches were flocking to these mountains to learn more about their powers. I glanced to Satarah, noticing the way her body stiffened as every eye turned to us. I placed my hand on her lower back, lending her some of my strength.

"Hello my witches. Thank you for coming when you were called. Alcyoneus and I have a few things that we want to share with you today." Satarah took a deep breath, "We have seven laws that we expect you to follow."

I took a deep breath, magic filling my chest as I projected my voice.

"One: A witch will never harm a human pure of soul.
Two: The Coven circle is sacred. Harming a member of your coven is forbidden.
Three: The powerful among you shall protect the weak or your blessed power shall be revoked.
Four: Bonded witches must never be kept apart. A bond is granted by us, and any who stand between them shall suffer our wrath.
Five: No witch shall ascend before their twenty fifth cycle. Magic is not for children.
Six. Any witch who calls upon us for help may be called upon at any time for our purposes.
Seven: We shall punish any who break our laws. No mortal soul will prevent our wrath."

As the magic faded, everyone was silent. We had spent hours discussing what rules our witches needed to follow to survive in the world. Parchment appeared in the hands of every witch in the crowd. No one would ever forget what we had decreed on this day.

Shouts filled my ears, questions flying in every direction. I growled at their insolence, but Satarah raised her hand and everyone became quiet, "We know that some of these may not yet make sense to you, but in time you will come to understand just how vital these rules will be to our survival. Today you will create the first covens, joining with your families and friends in a circle of power that cannot be broken. We will lead you, but you will look to your elders for guidance when we are not around." Her calm voice eased the tensions of the crowd, and I watched as magic flared. Groups paired off, various colors flaring around them as magic I did not understand came to life before our eyes. What Satarah and I had started would live on far longer than either one of us could truly comprehend. We watched hand in hand as the magic that Satarah had birthed grew in droves. Until before us stood thirteen groups. Thirteen different types of witches. The representations of the thirteen types of magic that lived inside of me and my wife. Only a small group stood closest to us, glowing in the deep purple that belonged to us.

So, thirteen covens were formed. *Blood, Sex, Shadow, Protection, Dream, Elemental, Siren, Spirit, Life, Death, Potion, Cosmic, and finally our small coven, Primal.* Mortals that were more like us, able to weave their will into the world without words or effort. It was a small group, but we would care for them. Slowly, the covens dispersed, laws in mind, and new purpose to seek. When only we remained, our coven disappearing into the village I turned to my wife, "You have changed the very face of the Earth, little star. Let us take our time enjoying it."

She took my hand, pressing her lips to my cheek as we made our way back into our small home. A small burden lifted from our shoulders.

Seven

Satarah

Decades passed us in the blink of an eye. The witches grew, expanding across the globe, covens popping up all over the Earth. Alcyoneus and I remained unchanged, unaged. Yet, our people gave us titles. We became the Mother and Father. The gods of the witches. The title brought me great joy, but also a sense of sadness. I wanted a child of my own, a beautiful being with the perfect mix of me and my husband. Yet no matter how much we tried I did not become pregnant. Alcyoneus had suggested magic, but I refused. If I was not meant to give him a child, then that would be my burden to live with. In the meantime, I doted on our witches. They were all our children in a way.

"We need to get away." Alcyoneus growled as he stepped into our small cabin. "The Blood Coven is driving me insane. I swear that new Priestess is just too happy."

I snorted, "She's too happy? You begrudge her for enjoying her life."

"I begrudge her for keeping me away from my beautiful wife." He responded, gathering me into his arms and kissing me fiercely. I melted into him, letting all of my thoughts disappear as we became one. When he lifted me up, moving our clothes out of the way so he could plunge his already hard cock into me I groaned. If we could live this way we probably would. Our bond thrummed as we joined, pleasure an afterthought as we stared into each other's eyes. I had always admired the purple of his irises, like the lavender that grows all over the mountains. No one else had eyes like that. I watched his eyes as he came, filling me with his seed. He still held me, continuing to pump in and out of me so slowly it was torture, "Today wife, I think I will live inside of you. I want to see just how many times I can fill your pussy with my seed before you beg for me to stop."

I laughed into his neck, "I never want to you anywhere else, my love, but we do have duties to attend to. All of the coven leaders will be here in a couple of hours for a meeting." It was true of course, I never tired of his cock, his fingers, or any of the ways he brought me pleasure and pain. It was a delicious mix that he had made me addicted to.

"Maybe they should see how well their dear Mother takes cock." He said. I felt his cock hardened again, and he began to slam into me with even more vigor. This time he carefully hit the spot inside of me that he knew would make me explode, "No, nevermind. They don't deserve to see any part of you." I couldn't think straight as he maneuvered my dress off my breasts, instantly taking one of my nipples into his mouth. It was too much, and I felt lightning down my spine as I came undone in his arms. Even as I shook, he didn't stop, relentlessly fucking me until he found his pleasure again. We were both panting as he sat down in one of the kitchen chairs, carefully slipping from inside me, "I just love to know you'll be dripping with my seed when you're talking to them."

"You're an awful man." I laughed, standing from his lap.

"And yet you chose to fall in love with me." He shot back.

I did, and it was the best decision I'd ever made. Had Alcyoneus not wandered into our forest I would have lived my days in loneliness with no purpose other than the small village I grew up in.

Instead, I'd found the other half of my soul. Together, we had built a community so vast it spanned across the world. Our witches weren't perfect, but they were the family I had created. Yet, I felt something changing and shifting within the world. Humans expanded every day, settling more and more of the land. Alcyoneus feared traveling like we once did, in fear that the humans who we ran into would tell others of the strange powers they encountered. We stood out in a way the rest of the witches did not. I'd come no closer to learning how we had come to roam this earth, but I'd decided long ago that I did not need those answers. The future was far more important than the past.

The elders were laughing and dancing as we looked on, spells flowing from their lips as they joined their power to work together. They did love each other's company, but I had insisted that it was not safe to gather often. What business we'd had was already concluded so they basked in the company of other powerful witches while we stood watch over them.

A sharp pain in my ear was the only warning we got as arrows began to rain down upon us. Shouts went up, but Alcyoneus was the first to move. His sword shimmered in the night as he went to hunt for whoever harmed us. Blood dripped down the side of my face as I searched for where the arrows came from. I ran into the center of the witches, forcing tears away when I noticed the elder of the Shadow coven had been shot through the heart. I called my magic, a glimmering shield forming on my arm. I fed it more magic forcing it to grow until it was large enough to protect all twelve of the remaining witches. "Stay here." I commanded them, shoving the magic shield into the dirt before them.

I followed the pulsing of my bond, feeling the rage that Alcyoneus could not contain. Yet there was a hint of fear I'd never felt from him before. It leaked down the bond, fueling my own anger as I came up on two of the humans who had dared to attack us. Without a thought I grabbed their spirits, yanking them from their bodies and sending them to the next realm. Their bodies thudded to the ground, but I continued moving aiming for where I felt my husband. When I stepped out of the trees my stomach dropped. Fires burned all around me, humans stood in a close-knit circle around an unlit bonfire. Alcyoneus was tied to the bottom of that bonfire, humans screaming at him. Blood ran down his face and even from this distance I could see the hate burning in his eyes. I could not understand why he stayed there, immobilized as they threw anything they could find at him. Some strange ropes glowed with a power I'd never seen before.

When a man stepped forward, a lit torch in hand I didn't think. I appeared before them all, "You will pay for your crimes here today." My voice rang out as I held up my hand. Magic flowed from me, shadows, fire, and vines combining to ripe these human's soul from their bodies. My unfettered power leaked out giving me a sense of peace until a sharp pain in my chest broke my concentration. The man with the torch had plunged a dagger into my heart. I fell backwards, landing in a heap at Alcyoneus' feet. He bellowed. Whatever had been holding him breaking under the sheer force of his rage. I gasped as every body in the area dropped. I could see their spirits disappearing one by one into the next realm. When there was no one to harm us, my husband dropped to his knees next to me.

"You will not die today." He commanded, "There is no one else who can save the humans from my wrath."

I coughed, blood splattering onto his white shirt, "You must care for our witches." My vision swam as I tried to take in one last look of Alcyoneus' face. His strong jawline was set in anger, unshed tears filled his purple eyes. His sorrow leaked down our bond, but I was unable to comfort him as pain wracked my body.

"I cannot live without you." He cried. It was the first time I'd ever seen him shed a tear, and I tried to lift my hand to comfort him. His pain shattered my already damaged heart. I opened my mouth to offer him solace, but before I could say anything everything went black.

Eight

Alcyoneus

Blood dripped from every inch of my body, but I didn't care. I had slaughtered every human within a hundred miles of my home. Had sent the witches away, sent them to give the message. They were now tasked with wiping all the filth from the earth. Any witch that came across a human soul that was unpure was duty bound to end their lives. My wife was dead, her body barely cold, and still I lived. Our bond was silent in my chest, the years of happiness we'd shared already quickly fading from my memory. I had not slept nor eaten in days, my single-minded task to end any who posed a threat to the people Satarah loved was the only reason I still stood. My heart was a lead weight in my chest without her. I had no purpose on this Earth without my wife by my side.

"Father, you must sleep." The Elder of the Dream Coven stood in the doorway of my home. Her hands on her slim hips. "This is not what the Mother would have wanted."

"I will cut you down where you stand, witch. Do not speak to me of what my wife would have wanted." I growled, pushing past her tiny body.

"Do you not feel the energy lingering? Sleep, Father. Answers lie in your rest." She said, cryptically. She disappeared before I could swing my sword at her neck.

I did not want to close my eyes and dream. I knew there was nothing but darkness in the corners of my mind that remained sane. Satarah had been the only balm for my soul. My greatest fear had come to life when that human had plunged his dagger into her chest. A world without her did not deserve to exist. I stripped of my clothes, scrubbing my skin off in the sink so I wouldn't sully the bed we'd shared. I found myself laying down, closing my eyes until I drifted off to sleep. Her scent still lingered on the sheets lulling me for the first time in weeks.

"Alcyoneus Alcyoneus! Where are you?" Satarah's voice penetrated my dreamless sleep. I sat up, taking in the strange surroundings I had found myself in. The world around me was a mix of blacks and purples, the only other light was the stars that hung above my head. I reached up wondering if I could touch them, instead the world shivered around me. "Alcyoneus!" I heard again, bringing me back to myself.

"Satarah! I'm here!" I shouted, standing and rushing toward her voice. It may have been dark, but the stars brightened slightly when I saw the white head of my wife. I ran faster, grabbing her into my arms the moment I was close enough, "I have missed you." I mumbled into her neck.

"And I you." She said, pulling away, "You have been busy with bloodshed." A smirk on her lips let me know that she was not angry. "Come we have much to discuss and very little time."

I allowed her to pull me further into the strange world we were in, until we came to a sprawling castle. I'd seen something like it in the old country, but it was still far larger than anything in the human realm. I gaped up at it as we approached, noticing the dark spirals that seemed to disappear into the sky. "It's beautiful, isn't it?" Satarah asked.

"Not as beautiful as you." I responded, taking her into my arms again.

"I created it. For us." She revealed, leaving me standing with my mouth agape.

"How?" That wasn't the most important question to ask, but it was the first thing to pop out of my mouth.

"We can't die." Satarah said, bringing my attention back to her face, "Yes, my body died in the way a humans would, but I still live. I have been trying to figure out a way back to the mortal realm, but without you I'm not powerful enough." I opened my mouth to ask another question, but she stopped me, "I still don't know exactly what we are, but we are somehow connected to the interworking's of the universe. We are needed for Earth to survive. I think together we could move between this plane and the next. Probably to any realm that exists."

The possibilities filled my mind, "How do I come to stay here? I want to be with you, away from the humans."

"It'll be our most powerful spell yet. You'll need to gather some potion ingredients on Earth first." A piece of paper appeared in her hand, "Take this. Find everything, we need. I will see you very soon, my love."

With a single kiss the dream began to fade. I held onto it long after I should have awoken.

It took me days to scour the earth for what Satarah had requested. Potion magic was not my strong suit. I'd never seen the point when I could do most anything with the snap of my fingers. I just hoped I could follow her instructions correctly. As the small iron pot boiled on the stove top I tossed in a small amount of each item; grape leaves, a deer antler, lavender, oak tree sap, sea water, my blood, and several other items I could not remember the names of went in. The brew swirled and bubbled before finally turning a dark purple. Slowly I poured it in a glass jar, before I stepped outside.

Coven elders stood impatiently, barely able to contain themselves as I made a path among them. I had only one focus, performing this spell so that I could be with Satarah again. I tuned out the questions and shouts as I began drawing a star pattern in the dirt, with magic I summoned each of the elements. Water, fire, earth, and air took up four of the points of the star. I moved to the fifth point, producing the glass jar. I raised it toward the coven and chugged it. The taste was awful, but the effect was instant, a swirling vortex of black and purple appeared in the center of the star. Everyone held their breath as Satarah stepped out from the vortex. Her white hair and silver eyes were complimented by the black dress she wore, "Children, thank you for gathering one last time. As you know, my mortal body was killed by humans. Because of their hatred I can no longer walk this world for long periods of time. Do not fret for I am always with you. Today the twelve of you will become our Priests. No longer simply elders, you will now guide your covens in our ways. When it is time we will select the new Priests, a crown upon their brow shall denote our favor. You will work our will upon this world, and we will bless you from our new realm." My eyes widened at her words. I did not know the changes that she had intended to make, but I appreciated them, nonetheless. "The Father will now join me in our new home but know that we are always close. All you have to do is call for us and we will answer your pleas. Remember the laws that we have given you." With those final words she turned to me, extending her hand. I took it without hesitation, stepping into the vortex.

I glanced out over the crowd, noticing the Protection coven elder, now the Protection Priestess stepping forward. Rain Dovey opened her arms wide, "My descendants and I will watch over these lands, we will keep your laws and memory alive." With those words she cast a spell, the golden shimmer of her magic slid over my skin just before the vortex began to close.

Satarah and I spoke at once, our voices echoing long after we were no longer in their realm, "Thank you, children. The Mother and Father will always be with you."

Nine

Satarah

For many, many years Alcyoneus and I were happy in the realm that belonged to us. We traveled the universe, finding no answers for our existence, but opening doors we had never thought to cross into. The land of the dead stretched before me now, a paradise in some places, and a place of repentance in others. All souls across the universe came here to rest.

"You can't be sure she will remember you." My husband said gently, "Magda died hundreds of years ago."

I ignored him as we walked through the fields of spirits. None of our people came here, instead we'd created a place in our own realm for the witches to stay after they passed on. We consumed the spirits of any who deserved our wrath, so all of our witches lived their afterlife in a paradise of our creation. I wanted to bring Magda to that place, so that we might visit her. I missed the woman who had raised me, even though I'd been without for more years than we'd had together.

"Satarah?" I spun around at the familiar voice.

"Magda?" Tears sprang into my eyes as I rushed toward the small spirit of the woman. I scooped her into my arms, tears running down my face as we embraced, "I've missed you so much."

"My sweet Satarah. I've missed you too. What are you doing here?" She asked.

Before I responded I took her in. She was younger here, more like how I remember her as a child, the only way to know she wasn't still alive was the faint glow that encompassed her body. "I'm here for you. I want to take you to my home."

She smiled, "I would love that."

I took her hand, motioning for Alcyoneus to hold her other hand. Together, we opened the vortex to our home. With both of us holding her we pulled Magda through with us. As we stepped out of the vortex, Magda gasped starting into the dark purple sky. "It's beautiful."

"This is our realm and your new home. We will escort you to where our witches roam once they've passed." I said.

"I can't stay with you?" She asked, "I thought we would be together again." I had not considered that she would want to live with us. Joy caused a smile to spread across my face.

I glanced to Alcyoneus, my heart squeezing. He nodded, and I sighed in relief, "We will set you up a room in the palace."

She grinned, taking my arm as we made our way to our home.

"You're happier with her here." Alcyoneus said as he entered our bedchamber.

"I am. It feels less lonely here with her. This is too much space for just the two of us." I admitted.

"Whatever makes you happy, wife." He said before he pounced on the bed, pinning my body to the mattress. "You'd better be quiet while I take you since Magda is just down the hallway."

My pussy pounded in time with my heart as he ripped the clothes from my body. He kissed my neck, slowly trailing his lips down my body until his head was between my legs. The first lick of his tongue at my core had me moaning loudly. His large hand clamped over my mouth as he chuckled, "I told you to be quiet, little star." His hand slapped down on my pussy, and I couldn't stop the muffled shout that left my covered mouth. "Ah ah, you're not listening." He continued to slap my most sensitive skin until I was silent behind his hand. He pulled his hand away but quickly replaced it with his cock. I gagged as he pressed deep into my throat forcing me to take every inch of him. "This will keep you quiet, won't it? You'll swallow every drop of my cum down that pretty little throat. Drown in it if you have to. All just to please me." I moaned, sucking harder. I snuck my hand toward my sore pussy, desperate for the orgasm I'd been denied, but he grabbed my hand. "Don't be a bad girl. I don't think your poor little pussy can take any more punishment." He slammed into my throat with more vigor, forcing me to gag around him until finally his hips stuttered his seed spilling down my throat. I drank every drop down greedily until he pulled away, grabbing my hips to lift me up as he laid in my spot. He arranged me until I was hovering over his face. He pulled my hips until he could latch onto my clit. I saw stars as he sucked and lapped at me. His hands roamed over the rest of my body, rolling my nipples in his fingers or prodding my ass until finally my orgasm crashed over me. I bit my lip to stop from shouting out.

As I climbed off of him, laying down to rest my head on his chest words left my mouth, "I want a child."

Alcyoneus was silent for a long time before he said, "I've never considered fatherhood. I'm not sure I could raise a child the right way, but if it is what you want then we will find a way."

"In all these years, I do not understand how I've never become pregnant." I said, sitting up.

"I don't know, little star, but we can make anything happen. Surely, we can find a way to have a child." He said, rubbing my back gently.

"You would be a great father, Alcy. I know you don't think you know how, but our witches worship you just as they do me. You are already a father in many ways." I said, kissing his cheek before I stood from the bed. "I'm going to the library. I want to read more on what the humans have learned about childbirth in the years we've been here."

"You aren't human, Satarah. They may not have the answers you seek." He pointed out.

I didn't respond as I blew him a kiss, wrapping a robe around my body before I left the room. The library was huge and constantly gaining more knowledge. Every book that existed on earth also existed in these four walls. A spell that Alcyoneus had worked for me in honor of our five hundredth anniversary. It was one of my favorite rooms in our home. I spent hours in here, reading everything from medical texts to stories of mythical creatures. The humans continued to thrive. Their thirst for knowledge leading them to so many discoveries. I had feared at one time that if they discovered my witches the persecution would begin again. Now it seemed that the humans might have begun to evolve away from their hateful and fearful mindsets. I hoped there was a future where humans and witches could live in harmony, working together against those with darkness in their souls.

Magda floated in distracting me from my thoughts, "Shouldn't you be resting?" I asked.

"The dead don't sleep, Satarah. Shouldn't you be resting?" She laughed as she took a seat next to me, peaking at the book in my hands, "You're trying to have a baby?" I nodded, unsure what to say, "That's wonderful, dear. You will make a great mother."

"I don't understand why I've never become pregnant." I admitted, closing the book, "We certainly do the right things to birth a child."

Magda looked off into the distance, considering for a long moment, "You and Alcyoneus are made of magic, maybe your child will also need to be created with magic." She stood, kissing my head, "Just remember, there is no rush. Things happen when they're meant to."

I considered her words for hours as I roamed the shelves. Magic was the lifeblood that created us, it stood to reason that our child would need magic to exist, but I didn't want to risk creating something different. Any child should be created in love, not power.

Ten

Alcyoneus

Our realm was overrun with witches and strange wolflike creatures I'd never seen before. At least seventy witches and warlocks cried out as they looked around at the strange realm, they had found themselves in after their deaths. I held up a hand to silence their cries, "Hush children. Magda will escort you to your final resting place." I had no idea why there had been an influx of souls today, but the stress that lined my shoulders only worsened when I saw Satarah rushing toward me.

"What's going on?" She asked. When she noticed the wolf creatures she let out a whistle that caused my ears to ring. Every one of them turned toward her, rushing to wait at her feet, "It's okay, little ones. Help Magda herd the souls to their proper place."

"What are those things?" I asked her, watching the way she gently petted one of them.

"I created them with my magic. I've been testing the limits to see exactly how will be best to work the spell for us to conceive." She admitted, pink filling her cheeks.

My wife was truly magnificent. Her power never stopped growing. I huffed a laugh, "Then I love them. Though I think we'd better figure out what is going on on Earth."

She nodded, turning in a flurry to enter our home. We stepped into the small dark room that we used to watch over our witches.

Only a wall sized mirror and two chairs took up the space. We had spent many hours in here, glasses of wine in hand as we forged the bonds that would lead our witches and warlocks to greatness. Together we tapped the mirror three times, the intention of our magic bringing up a clear picture. I was unsurprised to find us staring at the meeting hall of the Hex Guard. I'd had mixed feelings when the seven warlocks had banned together to bring more structure to the covens. Their intentions may have been pure, but they'd opened up the space for corruption. While our witches were more than humans, they were not like us, still mortal beings with the failings of mortal minds. Yet we had done nothing to stop them from forming. Now they had added new laws, things we would never have enacted. Coven registration sickened me the most. Our witches should form their covens organically. No warlock should have the power to deny those sacred bonds.

"We must end them. Their desire to follow the old ways is a threat to our power." One of the warlocks said as we tuned into their discussion.

Satarah stiffened at their words, but horror filled her face at the next words, "Our spell worked, Barbi Cruor has been eliminated. Garith has handled the Dovey coven. Slowly we will be able to dismantle the original covens. Once their influence is eliminated, we will have full control."

Rage filled my chest. I may not have the same motherly love for the witches that Satarah did, but they were still my children. No one would harm them without my wrath. I watched as image after image flashed through the mirror showing us all the corruption that we would be fighting. All of the original covens were in disarray, devastated by loss, filled with power hungry monsters, and much much worse. Yet I watched as Satarah took notes, unable to read the plan that was forming in her mind. My chest burned with the need to slaughter those that would harm all that we had built.

"I have to get to work." She finally said, deactivating the mirror. I tossed back the last of my fifth glass of wine, following her out of the room. "This is going to be the hardest fight of our existence, my love. Are you ready?"

"Let us remind them why they harkened us Mother and Father." I said.

There was never a time I wasn't in awe of my woman. The sheer power she contained should have had her worshipped as a god. Instead, she cared for our people with the heart and soul of a true mother. The lines of her body as she worked the spell were quivering with pent up rage. My cock responded to that in the most primal way. Tonight, I would take her, fill her with my seed and magic. Together we would create a child the universe had never seen before.

"Are you ready?" Satarah asked, turning her determined focus to me. I nodded, gathering magic into my chest as she made her way to me. She gave me no time to prepare, sliding down onto my cock as soon as I agreed. She rode me, harder than she ever had before, taking every inch of me into her pussy before pulling away. She spit onto my cock, muttering more words to her spell, before she slammed back onto me. My hands darted out, forcing her to stay in place. She struggled to maintain her voice as I set a grueling pace, slamming myself into her with enough force that her eye rolled back in her head. "We have to finish at the same time." She choked on a moan as I took one of her nipples into my mouth.

"Well, you better keep up, little star." I stood with her in my arms, careful not to disturb her markings. She wrapped her legs around my waist, allowing me plenty of leverage to fuck her the way that she liked. Once I saw her tittering on the edge I grabbed her hand, summoning my magic. She did the same, the silver of her eyes reflecting the purple of our magic as we finished her spell together. The feeling of our magic intensified the orgasm we shared, causing both of us to scream as dark purple light flared around us. I pulled her head to my chest, letting our magic fade as I held her, "No matter what happens next, I love you, Satarah. A child will not change an ounce of my obsession with you."

"I love you too, Alcyoneus. Thank you for giving me the chance to finally be a mother." There were tears in her eyes as she looked down at me.

"You know that the task you have set for our child will be more arduous than anything we have done, right?" I asked. My gut was twisted at the thought of sending our child to Earth to fix what we had allowed to become broken.

"We will set the path forward. They will not be alone." She responded, pressing a kiss to my lips before finally crawling out of my lap. I hated the loss of her skin against mine, but I turned to pull my black robe on. My mind drifted to Satarah's plan again. There were twelve daughters of the original covens roaming the earth, all of them very young, but already the power in them sang out to me. I closed my mind, imagining them once again. *Bambi. Larissa. Xava. Aislinn. Serafina. Electra. Catori. Lore. Amaya. Sage. Temple. Farah.* I repeated their names to myself constantly. These twelve witches would make or break our plan. If they were as powerful as we believed, they would help our child fix the world. If not, they would fail, and our witches could become extinct. We would be sending our child to their doom. They would not have the support of a Primal coven. The few Primal witches had died out hundreds of years ago, long before we'd left Earth. Mortal bodies just weren't meant for the unfettered power that Satarah and I shared.

Satarah's hand on my shoulder pulled me from my worries, "Let's go to bed, husband."

I grinned at the lust in her eyes. She was never sated. Even filled with my seed and our magic, Satarah craved me every bit as much as I craved her. At one time she may have been my prey, but now she was my entire world. If I had to choose between my wife and our witches, I would choose her every time. The world should hope that decision is never mine to make.

Epilogue

Satarah

My screams echoed off the stone walls of our room. Magda and Alcyoneus stood on either side of me, their words drowned out by the pain in my stomach. For ten months I had carried our child, now it seemed their birth would be my death. "I can't do it." I cried, as Magda wiped the sweat from my forehead.

"No child enters the world easily. This is the price that is demanded of all mothers." Magda said, "Even you are not spared from it."

I growled at her, but I knew she was right. I waved them away, shifting from my back to my hands and knees, "We're never having more children." I snapped at my husband as another contraction rocked my body.

"Whatever you desire, little star." He responded, placing one of his hands on my lower back, "Now let's finish this so we might meet our baby."

I nodded once, channeling all of my energy into another push. I felt the moment that my baby was finally born, a sense of relief flushing over me as tiny cries filled the room. Alcyoneus helped me sit back comfortably, and I felt his magic running over my body. Healing had never been a power either of us could master, but as his magic touched the damaged parts of my body, I felt them begin to stitch together. I sighed as the some of the pain subsided.

"Thank you." I muttered, too exhausted to keep my head up any longer.

I heard Alcyoneus coo over our child, "She has my eyes."

"It's a girl." I asked, forcing myself to sit up. I wanted to meet my daughter more than anything in the world. He took a seat next to me; our child already bundled tightly in his arms. As soon as I saw her small face tears began to run down my face, "She's perfect." Already her small head was full of soft, white curls. When her dark purple eyes met mine, I saw some sense of recognition pass behind them. I knew instantly that our daughter was different than any other mortal child. She was already aware, "We will name her Valterra."

"Valterra." Alcyoneus breathed, "My daughter you are the most loved creature in all of the universe."

I kissed her head, desperate to take her in my own arms. I adjusted myself until I could take her easily. Once she was in my arms, any anxiety or pain I'd been feeling vanished. Her small, wrinkled face was all I stared at for hours as Magda brought food, cleaned up the room, and ensured that we were comfortable.

"You need to rest, little star. I will take Valterra to her own room." Alcyoneus said, carefully lifting her away from me.

"Will you stay with her?" I asked, afraid of leaving her alone in the large castle.

"As if you even have to ask." He pressed his lips to my forehead before he disappeared.

I slept deeply for far too long, but I awoke rested. I climbed into a hot bath, cleaning myself quickly, before I went in search of my husband and my daughter. The scene that I stepped into was from a dream. Alcyoneus held Valterra against his chest, her white head and light pink outfit a contrast to his dark attire. His other hand he held a book that he read from quietly as he rocked her. Even from here I could tell that she was asleep, but that didn't stop him from continuing to speak, "This is one of your mother's favorite books. I thought we'd better start with something she likes, since everything I read is about war and death." He explained to her once he glanced down to see that she was asleep.

"She'll need to know about war before she goes to Earth." I pointed out, taking the opportunity to reveal myself.

His purple eyes roved over my body, taking in my healthy appearance. "Did you sleep well, little star?"

I nodded, "You could have woken me for a break."

"I will never need a break from my daughter." He responded, pressing a kiss to the top of my head as he passed me by, "She won't be going to Earth for a long, long time. I have plenty of time to teach her all the joys of killing a man. First, she will be a child."

My eyes misted over with tears. I had never seen such a soft side of him, even with all of his love for me, he had never tried to protect me from the truths of pain and death. No, we had reveled in those things together. Our daughter would not learn pain at our hands, instead we would raise her in so much love that Earth would rejoice when she came to deliver our witches and warlocks from corruption.

Once Valterra was in her crib Alcyoneus stood by my side, watching our precious baby sleep peacefully. "Are we doing the right thing?" I whispered, terrified to follow the plan I had created.

"We won't know for sure until the time has come." He admitted, reaching down to grab my hand, "I think this is how all mortals feel. We have something precious to lose in this battle, Satarah."

"We will not lose." I said, darkly, "We can't. Our witches are depending on us. Valterra depends on us."

"See how far you've come from that scared girl in the meadow, all those centuries ago? I never thought I could love you more until you brought our daughter into the world. I'll burn it all down for you. For her." Alcyoneus said, pressing a kiss to my lips.

He was right. We had fought through centuries to give our witches a world worth living. Now we would give our daughter the best chance to save it.

Acknowledgements

We're starting off with thanking my amazing Alpha team. I wrote this book in twelve days, with only sixish weeks before release they worked their butts off to make sure the best possible story went out to readers. Thank you, Emily, Karen, Shelby, Fern, Aleena, Edrie, Jordynn, Larissa, Laura, Presley, Samantha, Jetoria, Tina, Val and Zach. Your hard work, support, and dedication mean the world to me.

Leah... There's really not enough that I can say about how amazing my PA turned best friend truly is. Without you, I would never have made it this far in my writing career.

For my family and my fiancé... Seriously, the amount of bs y'all put up with so I can write and work full time is epic. Thank you for supporting my dreams.

To my ARC readers, the book only gets better when you get your hands on it! And for my street team... Seriously, my very favorite cuties.

And finally, to you, the reader. Without you, none of this means a thing. Thank you for giving this indie author a chance.

Also by

The Reclaiming Wonderland Series
Code Red
Code White: Frosted Wonderland
Blue Dreams
Emerald Knights (Coming Spring 2026)

The Austral Witches
Primal Echoes
One Bloody Night
Two Shadowed Hearts
Three Little Doves (Coming February 2026)

About the author

Taila has always had an obsession with stories, cultivated by a loving grandmother. She always had her nose in some book or another, but at fourteen she began writing her own stories. Code Red may be the first to publication, but you can expect many, many more to come. Taila lives in the hills of East Tennessee. Where she can often be found cuddling naughty kittens, reading, or working her day job. Occasionally, her family or partner will convince her to leave her cave to see the outside world.

If you want to chat with Taila or stalk the socials for book updates:

Facebook Page: Taila Cantrell Author

Facebook Group: Taila Cantrell's Cuties

Instagram: tcantrellauthor

TikTok: @tailatalks

www.ingramcontent.com/pod-product-compliance
Lightning Source LLC
Chambersburg PA
CBHW071136100726
47908CB00008B/2618